Picture books by the same author:

Alison and the Prince
I Forgot
A Witch Got on at Paddington Station
The Whales' Song

HARRY
and
CHICKEN

HARRY
and
CHICKEN

by
Dyan Sheldon
illustrated by
Sue Heap

CANDLEWICK PRESS
CAMBRIDGE, MASSACHUSETTS

For Harpo, Mao, and Elvis

Text copyright © 1990 by Dyan Sheldon
Illustrations copyright © 1990 by Sue Heap

First U.S. paperback edition 1994
First published in Great Britain in 1990
by Walker Books Ltd., London.

Library of Congress Cataloging-in-Publication Data

Sheldon, Dyan.
Harry and Chicken / Dyan Sheldon ; illustrated by Sue Heap.
Summary: Chicken adopts a stray cat, Harry, who is actually
an alien from the planet Arcana.
ISBN 1-56402-012-6 (hardcover)
[1. Cats—Fiction. 2. Extraterrestrial beings—Fiction.]
I. Heap, Sue, ill. II. Title.
PZ7.S54144Hap   1992   [Fic]—dc20   91-71851
ISBN 1-56402-275-7 (paperback)

10 9 8 7 6 5 4 3 2 1

Printed in Great Britain

Candlewick Press
2067 Massachusetts Avenue
Cambridge, Massachusetts 02140

CONTENTS

I Meet Harry

The day I met Harry, he was sitting on a trash can at the end of our road. It was raining, and his long gray hair was all flattened down. This made his eyes look about as big as the headlights on my dad's car. But Harry didn't look sad, or lost, or hungry, or anything like that. He was scrunched up on a can, complaining. I was walking by on my way home from school, and I heard this loud "Meow." I looked down, and there was Harry. Harry looked angry.

I thought that he was probably locked out and waiting for his owner to come home. I hadn't really paid much attention to him, but I had seen him on the street before. And once my father had found him sleeping on the roof of his car in the sun. "Will you look at that?" said my father. "Doesn't that take the cake?" But I didn't know where he belonged.

"What's the matter, boy?" I said. "Don't you like the rain?"

Harry gave me this look. It was the sort of look your mother gives you when she's busy and doesn't want you bothering her. I could tell right away that he was a special sort of cat. I could also tell that he wasn't very patient.

I tried again. I bent down and smiled so he'd know I wasn't going to hurt him. "What are you doing out here?" I asked. "Why don't you go home?"

Harry yawned. And then he gave me another one of his looks. This one said, "When are you going to stop wasting my time?"

I have one brother, Ben, and one sister, Lucy, but I'm the youngest. I can tell when I'm not wanted.

"Well, O.K.," I said. "Have it your own way. I was only trying to be friendly." I started to walk away.

And then I heard a voice behind me say, "Wait a minute, Chicken. Wait a minute."

I turned around. Nobody calls me Chicken except my family. They call me Chicken because I had a stuffed chicken I used to carry around with me everywhere when I was little. If I'd known I was going to get stuck with this stupid name, I would have carried something else—a stuffed deer or something—even being called Bambi would be better than Chicken. Nobody

else in the whole world is allowed to know that that's my nickname. Nobody. I never even told Kim. And Kim was my best friend, before she moved away.

I looked up and down the street, but there was no one around except the cat. I didn't know his name was Harry yet. "Who said that?"

Harry's ear twitched.

"Who do you think said it? The trash can?"

I looked over my shoulder. There was no one there. And then I looked up at the houses nearby. There were plants in the windows;

there were curtains in the windows; there was even old Bella the beagle in the Smiths' front window, sleeping as usual. But no people. No one who could talk. I looked at Harry. "You didn't say that, did you?" I asked.

Harry glanced at Bella. "Well it wasn't that dog, that's for sure," said Harry. He hadn't even met Bella yet, but already he didn't like her. *Typical Harry.*

"But cats can't talk." I said.

Harry jumped down from the trash can and stood at my feet. "Where I come from they can," he said.

"Oh," I said. I couldn't think of anything else to say. I was afraid to ask him where he came from, if you want to know the truth. I was afraid someone was going to come along, see me standing in the rain talking to a cat, and tell my mother that I was crazy or something.

Harry gave himself a little shake and looked up at me. "All right," he said. "I'm ready."

"Ready for what?"

"Ready to go home, of course," said Harry. We can't stand out here all day. I'll catch a cold."

"Wait a minute," I said. "You can't come home with me. My mother doesn't like cats."

Harry stretched.

"And my sister's allergic . . ."

Harry arched his back.

"And my brother has two birds . . ."
Harry yawned.
"And—"
Harry jumped into
my arms.
"I'm also hungry,"
he said. "I haven't
had a good
meal in

days." He snuggled up against me.

"Oh, are you?" I asked. But Harry was already falling asleep. I started walking home.

Harry's
Story

"So you see," said Harry, "there's no way of telling when I'll be able to go back."

Harry was sitting on my bed, stretched across my pillow. I'd dried him off with one of the towels from the bathroom, but there were still some little brown paw prints on my bedspread. My mother would have had a fit if she'd seen him. My mother is the enemy of dirt, mess, and animals on furniture.

"But it could be soon," I said. Next to Harry were the remains of the snack he'd just

eaten. He'd had a package of cream cheese, two sausages, a hard-boiled egg, and a bowl of cereal with milk. What remained was the plate and the bowl. "It could be today or tomorrow even."

Harry licked his mouth. "Or it could be years from now." The tip of his tail moved back and forth very slowly. "Nothing is predictable when you're dealing with time and space," said Harry.

You see, I'd been right when I thought that Harry wasn't an ordinary cat. In fact, he wasn't a cat at all. He was really an alien being from the planet Arcana. The creatures from the planet Arcana look a lot like sponges when they're at home. But when they travel in our solar system, they usually take on the form of a cat. Harry said that he liked being a cat. He said that cats

are beautiful, intelligent, and normal.

"What's more normal than a cat?" Harry wanted to know. "No one would ever think a cat was an extraterrestrial." (It wouldn't be long before I realized how true *that* was.)

Harry told me that he'd been visiting Earth for years and years. "Actually," said Harry, "I haven't been here for quite a while now." He looked thoughtful. "It used to be a lot nicer before it was so built up." He squidged up his nose.

"The air's not what it used to be."

This was the first time Harry had ever been to London. Or to the twentieth century. He looked out the window at the rain. "I'd always thought London would be a little damp for my taste," he said. "And I was right. Still, at least now I'll have a real chance to look around." He curled himself into a ball. "Get to know what life here is really like."

But how did Harry know about me? How did he know my name? It seems that he had been watching me for weeks. He followed me to school and home again, he followed me to the mall and on my paper route. On weekends he would sit under the bushes in the garden and listen to my family talking. At night he would sit on the birdbath in the garden and watch us through the window.

"You know what, Chicken?" said Harry. "I knew the minute I first saw you that we were going to be friends." He rolled over on his other side.

"You mean even before your ship disappeared?" What had happened was that Harry's spaceship had vanished into thin air. Apparently

this is something that happens to Arcanan space-ships all the time. Harry says it is a flaw in the design.

"Of course," said Harry, "you and I were destined to be friends. Who else would I turn to in my hour of need?"

"Can't they just beam you up or something?" I asked. "Can't they just rescue you?"

Harry sighed. "I'm afraid not. I've heard of Arcanans being stranded for centuries."

I looked around my room. It already seemed crowded with Harry in it. I wasn't sure how long

I was going to be able to keep him a secret. My mother had watched me in a funny way when I was making Harry's snack. What had I done with my lunch? Why didn't I go out and play? Why did I want to sit in my room eating all afternoon? Hadn't I made any new friends yet? Was I missing Kim?

"Centuries?" I repeated. "You mean you might be stuck here for centuries?"

"Exactly," said Harry. His nose twitched. "Is there anything more to eat?"

Harry couldn't live in my room for centuries. My mother was always coming in and making sure that I hadn't left my socks on the floor and things like that. My sister and brother were always barging in. My father always came up to kiss me good night.

"No, there's no more to eat," I snapped at him. "You've had it all. Do you really mean you might be here for centuries?"

Harry rolled onto his back. "Yes," he said. "So you see, it's lucky I found you."

I looked at Harry, lying there with his head on my pillow and his paw on my mother's favorite plate. There were crumbs everywhere. He was making this strange sound that was something like a purr and something like the hum of a refrigerator.

"Oh, yes," I said. "Very lucky."

Harry
Gets
Lost

"I think I'll have a little catnap," said Harry. He walked in a circle and then lay back down exactly where he'd been. "After I've rested I'll take a look around."

"You'll do no such thing," I said. "I told you, if you want to stay here, you're going to have to stay hidden."

"Oh, pooh pooh," said Harry. "You take things too seriously, Chicken. Where would I be if I worried about everything the way you do?"

"Safe at home in Arcana," I said. But Harry's eyes were already shut tight.

He slept on my bed all afternoon. I wasn't going to tell him, but it was nice having him snoring behind me. I suppose I just liked having a friend around. Even if it wasn't Kim but a cat from another planet!

While Harry napped, I sat at my desk, pretending to do my homework. What I was really doing was staring out at the rain and wondering what I was going to do. I mean, I couldn't keep him, could I? No matter how careful I was, sooner or later someone was going to find out he was there.

Harry said it didn't matter that my sister was

allergic to cats because, since he wasn't a real cat, she wouldn't be allergic to him. Harry said that it didn't matter that my brother had two birds because, since he wasn't a real cat, he wasn't going to hurt them, was he? Harry said it didn't matter that my mother didn't like cats. She would like him.

I thought it might be true that Harry wouldn't make my sister sneeze and break out in a rash. And it might be true that Harry wouldn't try to make bird sandwiches out of Madonna and Rambo. But it wasn't true that my mother was going to like Harry. Harry didn't know my mother. If she said she didn't like cats, that meant all cats, forever and ever.

I doodled on my math notebook. Harry snored.

On the other hand, I couldn't throw Harry out, could I? Where would he go? What would he do? He couldn't live on the street like a stray. He didn't like sleeping on trash cans and window ledges. He hated being cold and wet. He wasn't too thrilled about eating garbage either. Besides, out on the street he might get run over. Or stolen. You were always reading in the paper about people stealing cats to experiment on or to make coats from their skins. Harry was a guest on our planet. As a human being I had a responsibility to make sure that he was treated well. Didn't I?

I stared across the street to where Kim used to live. What would Kim say if she were still here and not in Manchester? Kim would say that I had to help Harry. "No problem, Sara," she'd say. "Easy peasey." But *then* what would Kim say? That she'd help hide Harry? That I should cry and throw myself on my parents' mercy? That I should tell my parents the truth? That was the part I had trouble with—working out what Kim's "easy peasey" solution would be.

Then my mother called me for supper.

"Coming, Mom!" I shouted. And I turned to the bed to tell Harry that I had to leave him for a while.

Harry wasn't there.

"Harry?" I said. I looked over at the door, but it was still shut. "Harry? Harry, stop messing around. Where are you?"

I looked under the bed. No Harry.

I looked in the closet. No Harry. I looked behind my desk and my dresser. Unless he'd turned

himself into a pencil or a ball of dust, he wasn't there either.

"Come on, Harry," I said. "Where are you?" Then I remembered that cats like to get into things. So I checked all the drawers. And the waste-paper basket. And my knapsack.

There were little brown paw prints that went straight across the carpet and ended at the door. I had to face the terrible truth. Harry wasn't in my room at all. Somehow or other, he had gotten out. Even though I had warned him. Even though I had told him he had to stay hidden. I went to the door and opened it. There was no Harry on the landing. No Harry at the top of the stairs. I looked in the linen closet. No Harry. I looked in the bathroom. I looked in the bathtub.

I looked in the laundry basket. I checked under the sink. No Harry. He could be anywhere, I told myself, knowing how curious cats are. He could be in Lucy's room. Or in the junkyard Ben calls his room. He could be behind the curtains in the living room. Or in the room where my mother made her pottery, and he might be covered with clay.

"Chicken!" shouted my mother. "Chicken! What's taking you so long?"

"I'm coming!" I yelled back. "I'm coming."

Or he could be in the kitchen, where, right at that moment, everyone was sitting down to eat.

Things
Start to
Go
Wrong

Supper went on for hours. Everybody was eating really slowly and talking and talking. You'd think they were planning to sit there till morning.

"You're very quiet tonight, Chicken," said my father. "Didn't anything interesting happen to you today?"

But I was busy looking around the room for some sign of Harry. Could he be in the oven? I wondered. Could he be in the broom closet?

"Sara Jane," said my father. "I asked you a question. Did anything interesting happen to you today?"

"You mean at school?"

My brother laughed. "No, dumbo. While you were swimming the English Channel."

My sister smirked. "The only interesting thing that ever happened to Chicken was the time she got lost."

"Ben," said my mother. "Lucy. That's enough."

"No," I said. I stabbed my twentieth pea with my fork. I like to eat my peas one at a time. "It was pretty quiet."

"I wish you'd tell her to stop playing with her food," said Lucy. "What if we had visitors?"

"I knew you wouldn't be hungry now," said my mother. "Not after all that food you ate this afternoon."

My father looked at my mother. "What's this?"

"You should have seen the snack this girl had when she got home today," said my mother. "You'd have thought she hadn't eaten for days."

"You're right," I sighed. "I'm really full. And I have a lot of homework. Can I be excused?"

My mother gave me one of her mother looks. "You just stay right where you are, young lady," she said. "You know the rules." The first rule is no eating between meals. The second rule is nobody leaves the table until everyone is finished. The first rule meant I was going to have trouble sneaking food for Harry. The second rule meant I wasn't going to have a chance to look for him until everybody was in bed.

I helped clear the table. Harry wasn't in the cabinet, or the sink, or the fridge.

"Chicken," said my mother. "What are you looking in the oven for?"

"Me? Nothing." He wasn't in there either.

My mother started toward the pantry. "Just wait till you see what we've got for dessert," she said to my father. "Your favorite! Apple crisp." She had a big smile on her face.

The pantry! Of course! That was where my

mother kept the butter and the cheese. That was where my mother would have the jug of cream waiting for the crisp. That was where I would find Harry.

I shot past her. "I'll get it, Mom," I said. "You've been working all day. You sit down and rest."

"Oh brother," said Ben, pretending to choke. "Now I've heard everything."

My mother gave me another mother look. "Sara Jane Thomas," she said, "just what has gotten into you?"

But I was already at the door of the pantry. Please, I prayed. Please make him be in there. Make him be in there and sound asleep in a corner where no one will see him.

I opened the door.

No Harry. I looked again. Oh no. What had I done to deserve this? There was no Harry. There was no cream. There was no apple crisp. There was an empty cream jug, on its side. There was an empty apple crisp dish, licked clean. There was a wedge of cheese with teeth marks in it.

"Hurry up, will you, Chicken?" Lucy yelled. "We're waiting."

"Come on, honey," my father shouted. "Shake a leg."

Shake a leg? I couldn't even move one toe.

My mother came up behind me. She put a hand on my shoulder. "Sara, what are you doing in here?" she asked. And then she sort of screamed. "Oh my goodness! John! John! Come and look at this!"

Everyone rushed into the pantry. "It must have been thieves," said Ben. Lucy thumped him. "Don't be stupid. Thieves don't take the apple crisp and leave the television."

"It must be some sort of animal," said my mother.

I tried to look surprised. "Do you think so?" I asked. "An animal? How would an animal get in here?"

"That's a very good question," said my father, looking right at me.

"Maybe we have rats," I suggested.

My father held up the cheese. "Do these look like rat teeth marks to you?"

"Gosh, Dad," I said. "You know, I really think they do."

Harry
Hits New
Heights

Harry was up a tree.
I saw him when I was
getting ready for bed.
I went to my window
to draw the curtains,
and there, right in front
of me in my mother's
prize maple tree, was
Harry. He did not
look happy.

I opened the window. "Harry!" I cried. "Harry, what are you doing up there?"

"I'm waiting for a bus, of course," said Harry, all huffy. And then he sort of looked away. "If you must know," he said, "that creature with the short legs and the long ears and no brain chased me up here."

Bella, the Smiths' beagle. Bella hates cats.

"Harry," I hissed. "Harry, you've got to come back inside."

Harry turned his back to me. "Chicken," he said, "I would love to come back inside. But I don't seem to be able to get down." He flicked his tail. "I'm going to need a little help."

In stories when a cat gets stuck up a tree, the fire department comes and gets it down. That's it. Easy peasey, as Kim would say. All the cat's owner has to do is call the fire department and then go and stand on the lawn. Then the fire engine comes, and a nice fireman gets out and starts climbing the tree. The cat's owner stays on the ground and acts grateful.

But not me.

First I had to wait about a million years for my parents to go to bed so I could sneak downstairs. And then I had to *get* downstairs. Have you ever noticed that everything sounds louder in the dark? Even though I was hardly breathing as I crept along, it sounded like a horse going down the stairs. Any minute I expected to hear my mother behind me, shouting, "Sara Jane! Sara Jane! Did you bring that horse into the house?"

And everything looks different, too. The hat stand looked like a man. The pile of stuff on the hall table looked like a monster. Every shadow looked like a rat. I must have had about fourteen heart attacks before I finally got to the front door.

And then, after all that, I had to climb up a stupid old tree in the middle of the night. At least it had stopped raining.

"Hurry up, Chicken," Harry kept saying. "I'm getting cold up here."

Climbing trees is not easy when you're in your bathrobe, pajamas, and hippopotamus slippers. But at least if my mother caught me, I could pretend that I'd been sleepwalking.

"I'm coming as fast as I can, Harry," I grunted. "It's not my fault you don't know how to get down from a tree."

Harry didn't say anything to that. He just stared down at me with his enormous yellow-green eyes. It was sort of spooky.

"O.K.," I said. "I'm coming. I'm coming."

What also happens in the stories is that the cat that is stuck in the tree is very sweet and well behaved. When the fireman picks it up, the cat sort of snuggles against him and purrs. The cat does not get all hysterical and dig his claws into the fireman's shoulder. The cat does not immediately start complaining.

"You're holding me all wrong," grumbled Harry. "Don't hold me so tight."

"Harry!" I practically screamed. "Pull your claws in. You're hurting me."

Harry hit my face with his tail. Hard. "Watch where you're going, Chicken, you almost slipped. Chicken, be careful! That branch nearly hit me."

He was wrapped around my neck like a scarf. I could hardly breathe, let alone see. At the rate we were going, we'd still be in this tree when morning came.

"Harry," I said. "You are going to have to calm down. I can't do this with you moaning the whole time and tearing my shoulders apart."

"I am not moaning," said Harry. His tail whacked me in the mouth. His claws dug another inch into my skin. "And I am always calm."

The branch we were on started to wobble. Harry shifted his body so that he was sort of draped over my head.

"Harry!" I cried. "Harry, watch what you're doing. I can't . . . Harry . . . !"

And something snapped.

The lights went on in my parents' room.

We'd landed in the bushes under their window. "Shhh," I said to Harry. He was a little shaken, but otherwise all right. I had a few

scratches on my arms, but they were from Harry.

We could hear my parents talking through the open window. Well, we could hear my mother talking.

"John," my mother said. "John, did you hear something?"

My father made a noise.

"John," said my mother. "Wake up! I think I heard someone outside."

And then my father, sounding really sleepy, said, "I didn't hear anything, Marilyn. Go back to sleep."

"John," said my mother. "John, I think you should go and look."

"Honestly, Marilyn. It's one in the morning."

"John, I heard something, I tell you. I'm sure I did. Go and look."

There was the sound of someone banging into something and a shout of pain. Then my father's head appeared at the window.

Harry and I held our breath.

"Nothing there," said my father. And he slammed the window shut.

"Whew," I whispered to Harry. "That was close."

Harry shook himself. "No thanks to you," he said.

"No thanks to me? You're a fine one to talk. What about you? You're the alien. You're supposed to have special powers. You're supposed to be able to fly and make things move and stuff like that."

"You watch too many movies, Chicken," sniffed Harry. "I'm an extraterrestrial, not a magician. You should try to remember that."

"Right, Harry," I said, as I picked him up and started sneaking back into the house. "I'll remember."

My Mother Worries about Me

I was woken up by Lucy shouting. "Chicken! Chicken! Mom says you've got to get up. You can't stay in bed all day just because it's Saturday."

I rolled over. There was something furry tickling my nose. Harry. For a second I'd forgotten about him. "I'm coming," I shouted back. "I'll be right there."

She started rattling the doorknob. "Hey, what's this? You've locked the door."

"I'm entitled to a little privacy."

"Oooh, pardon me," said Lucy. I could hear her stomping away.

Harry opened one eye and yawned. "Breakfast time?" he asked.

By the time I got downstairs there was no one in the kitchen except my mother.

"Well," she said, "you're certainly a sleepyhead this morning."

I said, "Um."

"And what's this about locking your door?"

I poured myself some fruit juice. "Lucy and Ben are always barging into my room." Which is the truth. "Sometimes I like to be alone, too, you know."

That was the wrong thing to say. Since Kim left, my mother thinks I'm alone too much. She made one of her mother sighs.

"Wow," I said, changing the subject. "I'm really hungry. Can I have two boiled eggs and bacon and toast and maybe a couple of sausages?"

My mother looked at me as if she were going to take my temperature. "You seem to be very hungry all of a sudden."

"I am," I said. "I'm very hungry. It must be because I'm growing." I reckoned that if I got two of everything, I could slip one into my pocket for Harry and maybe stop him from getting into the pantry again. Not that he was going to go wandering for a few hours at least. I was sure he'd learned his lesson after being stuck in that tree half the night. I started pouring myself a bowl of cereal. "Look," I said, "I'm starving."

My mother turned to the stove. She cleared her throat. "Now, Chicken," she said. "I don't want you moping around the house like you have been for the past few weeks. Just because Kim's not here doesn't mean that there's nothing for you to do." She started banging pans around.

"I've been a little worried about you lately, you know. Sleeping late. Staying in your room by yourself all the time." She pointed out of the window with her slotted spoon. "There's a great big world out there, you know. It's time you went out and saw it."

"I'm only ten years old, Mom," I said. "Do you want me to leave home?"

"You know what I mean," said my mother. She put two pieces of toast in front of me. "In fact, I'll tell you what. Why don't you and I do some shopping today? We'll go up to the shopping mall. We can even have lunch out."

Normally, I like going to the mall and eating out and everything. But today I sort of wanted to keep an eye on Harry. I started buttering my

toast. "Well, I don't know, Mom. I've got quite a few things I want to do today."

"Like what?" said my mother.

"Like what?"

"Yes. Like what? What do you have to do today that's so important?"

"Well . . . um . . . homework." My mother's a great believer in homework.

"Homework?" she said, as though it were the most ridiculous thing she'd ever heard. "But you were in your room for hours yesterday doing homework."

"Because I've got so much. I—"

"Don't be silly," said my mother. "All work and no play makes Sara Jane a dull girl."

Just then my father came in, carrying a large branch. "You were right, Marilyn," he said to my mother. "You did hear something last night. Look at this. It was broken off the maple tree."

My mother immediately became emotional. "Oh, no! My maple tree! How did that happen?"

"From the look of it, I'd say something pretty heavy must have been sitting on it."

"On our tree? In our garden?" While she was shrieking at my father, I wrapped a piece of toast in a napkin and slipped it off the table. "But what?"

"I'm not sure," said my father. He looked over at me. "I wonder if it could have been one of Chicken's rats."

Harry
Meets
My Mother

Harry didn't want to stay behind while I went shopping with my mother.

"I get bored, Chicken," he said, chewing on his eggshell. "It isn't any fun being all by myself."

"Harry," I explained, "nobody takes a cat shopping. And anyway it gets really crowded on Saturdays. You'd hate it."

"I wouldn't hate it," Harry protested. "I'm interested in the way people live today."

"Believe me, you'd hate it. It's just a whole lot of people pushing and shoving and lugging shopping bags around."

"All right," said Harry. "I'll wait for you in the car."

"Forget it, Harry," I said. "The car is hot and stuffy. You'd have to hide the whole time. You'd really *really* hate that."

Harry finished licking the butter off his toast. "But not as much as I'd hate being alone."

So, against my better judgment, I hid Harry under a blanket in the back of the car where all

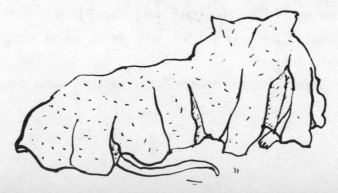

the junk is. "You just stay there and be quiet," I warned him as I tucked his tail in. "Understand?"

Harry's muffled voice floated from under the cover. "Of course I understand."

"What a perfect afternoon," said my mother. "Aren't you glad you came?"

We'd already covered the entire lower level. I collapsed onto the nearest chair in the restaurant. "I'm having a great time," I said. And I was. I'd forgotten how much fun the shopping mall could be. And how nice it was to spend time with my mother. In fact, I was having such a great time that I hadn't thought about Harry at all.

My mother sat down and looked around. "I do think this must be one of the prettiest malls anywhere. And so peaceful. Not like shopping in the city."

"It's terrific," I agreed. We were sitting at the window. I pointed across the way. "I like the fountain." The fountain was huge. It was surrounded by a beautiful blue pool, filled with water lilies.

"And so many stores," my mother went on.

"You hardly know where to begin." She picked up her menu. "Well," she said happily, "shall we order some lunch?"

I was just putting the ketchup on my hamburger when my mother suddenly said, "What's that?"

"What's what?"

"That sound."

"I can't hear anything," I said.

"Shh," said my mother. "Listen. It's coming from outside."

There were one or two people at the other tables who looked as though they had heard it too. But all I could hear were voices and the music that was playing in the background.

"What does it sound like?"

My mother frowned. "Well, I'm not quite sure."

Several guards hurried past the window.

"It sounds like a race," said my mother.

"A race? In the Millwood Shopping Mall?" I laughed.

She looked nervously out of the window. "Well, maybe not a race, but running. I can definitely hear people running."

Some of the other customers were getting up and going to the door.

"Maybe it's joggers," I suggested. "You know, advertising track suits or sneakers or something."

"I can hear shouting too," said my mother. "Joggers don't shout, they just grunt now and then."

The music stopped suddenly.

I put some French fries on top of the ketchup on top of my hamburger and closed the bun. "Happy shoppers?" I asked. "Happy shoppers hurrying to a sale?"

"Not shouting," said my mother. "Yelling and screaming."

I bit into my burger. "Unhappy shoppers?"

My mother looked confused. "Can't you hear it, Chicken? I'm sure it's getting louder."

But it was hard to hear anything now because there were so many people standing outside the restaurant, pointing and making a lot of noise.

For some reason, I was starting to feel a little nervous myself. I stood up for a better view. Everyone was staring at the second level. I stared at the second level. There were stores. There were people. Nothing out of the ordinary. And then I saw it.

It was a big gray cat. He was racing along the second level. He had a pair of fancy silk underpants wrapped around him. He had a pizza in his mouth. The running sound came from all the people who were racing after him. It looked like there were hundreds of them. They were yelling

and screaming and shaking their fists. The cat
looked sort of upset. He stood for a second looking down at the fountain. His yellow-green eyes
were enormous.

"Oh no!" I screamed. "Harry!" And I jumped
up from the table and ran outside.

My mother ran after me.

But the cat had disappeared. The people who
had been chasing him were leaning over the rail-
ings, looking down; and all the people who had
been watching them chase him were standing on
the ground floor looking up.

"Well, can you beat that?" said the man next to us. "Where did he go?"

"He must have jumped into the pool," said his wife.

"In the pool?" The man laughed. "Cats hate water."

"Cats can't swim," said another man.

"They can swim," said someone else, "but they can't dive."

"Dive!" several people shouted together. "Did you see any splash?"

Nobody had seen a splash. And nobody seemed to have noticed the large mushroom pizza floating among the water lilies.

"Maybe it was one of those hologram things," said a woman behind me.

"Sara Jane," shouted my mother. "Sara, where do you think you're going?"

I squeezed my way to the edge of the fountain.

And there, just peering over the edge of the pizza, was what I was looking for.

I pulled him out of the water and wrapped him in my jacket.

"What in the world is that?" asked my mother, coming up beside me. Several angry salespeople had come up beside me too.

"This is Harry," I said. There wasn't much else I could say.

"Whose cat is that?" screamed a man in a white apron, shaking his fist.

"He's my cat," I said, not looking at my mother.

Harry started to snore.

Harry's
Fate
Is
Decided

Harry said that the trip to the shopping mall was the worst thing that had happened to him in at least three hundred years. My mother more or less agreed with him. The first thing she said to my father when we got home was, "You talk to her."

My father made one of his "uh oh" faces. Uh oh, now what have you done?

In the end, they both talked to me. I decided to tell them the truth.

"I just don't understand, Sara Jane," said my mother. "Where did this cat come from?"

"I told you, I found him out by the Smiths' garbage cans. He comes from another planet."

My mother looked over at my father. "Right. And how did he get to the mall?"

"I brought him with us in the car."

"But you're usually so sensible. Why would you do something so foolish?"

I looked at Harry, who was wrapped up in a blanket, sound asleep on my lap. "I didn't want him to get lonely."

My father looked at my mother. "You didn't want him to get lonely?"

"No."

"How considerate of you, Sara."

My mother folded her hands in front of her.
"And how, if you locked him in the car, did he
end up in the pizza parlor?"

"Mom," I said, "you're not listening to me.
Harry can do things like that. He's got special
powers."

"Yes, I've seen some of those," said my mother. "Thank goodness the damage wasn't too bad this time. One large pizza with double cheese and mushrooms and a pair of under-pants."

"He was hungry," I said. I decided not to mention that he was always hungry. "And then that man started yelling, and he frightened Harry. Can you imagine how upset he was when all those people started chasing him?" I put on my saddest expression. "The poor little thing," I sighed.

My mother looked over at Harry. "Yes," she said in that doubtful, mother way of hers. "The poor little thing."

I patted Harry's head. "You can see how much all this excitement has exhausted him. He comes from a much more peaceful planet."

My father smiled. "Arkansas, is it?"

"Arcana."

"Where he really looks like a sponge." His smile became wider.

"Something like a sponge." I was beginning to suspect they didn't believe me.

My mother and father looked at each other again.

"Sara," said my mother at last. "If you wanted a pet to keep you company, why didn't you just ask us? Why concoct this incredible story?"

"But I haven't concocted it. It's true. And anyway, if I'd asked, you would have said no."

My mother's eyebrows went up. "How do you know that if you didn't ask?"

"Because you always said that you don't like cats."

My mother glanced over at Harry. He was looking pretty handsome now that he'd dried off. "I don't remember ever saying any such thing," said my mother. "I will admit I've never been overly fond of them . . ."

I looked from my mother to my father. "Does this mean I can keep him?"

"Well," said my father. "There are a few rules."

"You mean I can keep him?"

"The first rule," said my mother, "is that he is totally your responsibility. Do you understand?"

"Absolutely."

"The second rule," said my father, "is that he stays out of the pantry and out of trouble. No more helping himself to apple crisp."

"Dad!" I looked shocked.

My father wasn't moved. "No more climbing in your mother's maple tree," he said sternly.

I decided not to waste my breath protesting. "No problem."

"The third rule," said my father, "is that he doesn't bother Lucy."

"Of course. Of course. He won't bother Lucy. You'll see. She won't even be allergic to him because he's not a real cat."

My father looked at my mother. My mother looked at my father.

"And that," said my mother, "is the fourth rule."

"What is?"

"We don't want to hear any more of this alien visitor story. Is that clear?"

"But—"

"Is that clear, Sara Jane?"

I looked down at Harry. He was smiling in his sleep. "Yes, Mom. That's perfectly clear."

"What's that awful noise?" asked my father.

"It sounds like a broken helicopter."
"That's Harry," I said. "He's purring."

Don't miss another
Harry and Chicken adventure:
Harry the Explorer